Alessandro Baricco was born in Turin in 1958. He is the author of thirteen novels, as well as a number of essay and short story collections, a modern rendition of *The Iliad* and a theatrical monologue. He has won the Prix Médicis Étranger in France and the Selezione Campiello, Viareggio and Palazzo al Bosco prizes in Italy.

Ann Goldstein is a frequent translator from Italian. She has translated works by, among others, Elena Ferrante, Pier Paolo Pasolini, Alessandro Baricco, Erri De Luca and Roberto Calasso.

Selected works in translation by Alessandro Baricco

The Young Bride
Three Times at Dawn
Mr Gwyn
Emmaus
Without Blood
An Iliad
City
Ocean Sea
Lands of Glass

ALESSANDRO
BARICCO

Translated from the Italian by Ann Goldstein

CANONGATE

This Canons edition published in Great Britain in 2019 by
Canongate Books

First published in Great Britain in 2006 by Canongate Books Ltd,
14 High Street, Edinburgh EH1 1TE

canongate.co.uk

1

The publisher gratefully acknowledges subsidy from the Scottish Arts
Council towards the publication of this volume

This English translation was supported by the Italian Cultural
Institute, Edinburgh

EDIMBURGO

British Library Cataloguing-in-Publication Data
A catalogue record for this book is available on
request from the British Library

ISBN 978 1 78689 642 1

Typeset by Palimpsest Book Production Limited, Falkirk, Stirlingshire

Printed and bound by CPI (UK) Ltd, Croydon CR0 4YY

MIX
Paper | Supporting
responsible forestry
FSC
www.fsc.org   FSC® C171272

I.

ALTHOUGH his father had imagined for him a brilliant future in the army, Hervé Joncour ended up earning his living in an unusual profession that, with singular irony, had a feature so sweet as to betray a vaguely *feminine* intonation.

For a living, Hervé Joncour bought and sold silkworms.

It was 1861. Flaubert was writing *Salammbô*, electric light was still a hypothesis and Abraham Lincoln, on the other side of the ocean, was fighting a war whose end he would not see.

Hervé Joncour was thirty-two years old.

He bought and sold.

Silkworms.

2.

To be precise, Hervé Joncour bought and sold silk-worms when the silkworms consisted of tiny eggs, yellow or grey in colour, motionless and apparently dead. Merely in the palm of your hand you could hold thousands of them.

'It's what is meant by having a fortune in your hand.'

In early May the eggs opened, freeing a worm that, after thirty days of frantic feeding on mulberry leaves, shut itself up again, in a cocoon, and then, two weeks later, escaped for good, leaving behind a patrimony that in silk came to a thousand yards of rough thread and in money a substantial number of French francs: assuming that everything happened according to the rules and, as in the case of Hervé Joncour, in a region of southern France.

Lavilledieu was the name of the town where Hervé Joncour lived.

Hélène that of his wife.

They had no children.

3.

To avoid the devastation from the epidemics that increasingly afflicted the European stock, Hervé Joncour tried to acquire silkworm eggs beyond the Mediterranean, in Syria and Egypt. There lay the most exquisitely adventurous aspect of his work. Every year, in early January, he left. He traversed sixteen hundred miles of sea and eight hundred kilometres of land. He chose the eggs, negotiated the price, made the purchase. Then he turned around, traversed eight hundred kilometres of land and sixteen hundred miles of sea, and arrived in Lavilledieu, usually on the first Sunday in April, usually in time for High Mass.

He worked for two more weeks, packing the eggs and selling them.

For the rest of the year he relaxed.

4.

'WHAT'S Africa like?' they asked.

'Weary.'

He had a big house outside the town and a small workshop in the centre, just opposite the abandoned house of Jean Berbeck.

Jean Berbeck decided one day that he would never speak again. He kept his promise. His wife and two daughters left him. He died. No one wanted his house, so now it was abandoned.

Buying and selling silkworms, Hervé Joncour earned a sufficient amount every year to ensure for him and his wife those comforts which in the countryside people tend to consider luxuries. He took an unassuming pleasure in his possessions, and the likely prospect of becoming truly wealthy left him completely indifferent. He was, besides, one of those men who like to *witness* their own life, considering any ambition to *live* it inappropriate.

It should be noted that these men observe their fate the way most men are accustomed to observe a rainy day.

5.

IF he had been asked, Hervé Joncour would have said that his life would continue like that forever. In the early Sixties, however, the pebrine epidemic that by now had rendered the eggs from the European breeders useless spread beyond the sea, reaching Africa and even, some said, India. In 1861, Hervé Joncour returned from his usual journey with a supply of eggs that two months later turned out to be almost entirely infected. For Lavilledieu, as for many other cities whose wealth was based on the production of silk, that year seemed to represent the beginning of the end. Science appeared incapable of understanding the causes of the epidemic. And the whole world, as far as the farthest regions, seemed a prisoner of that inexplicable fate.

'*Almost* the whole world,' Baldabiou said softly. 'Almost', pouring a little water into his Pernod.

6.

BALDABIOU was the man who, twenty years earlier, had come to town, headed straight for the mayor's office, entered without being announced, placed on the desk a silk scarf the colour of sunset, and asked him

'Do you know what this is?'

'Women's stuff.'

'Wrong. Men's stuff: money.'

The mayor had him thrown out. He built a silk mill, down at the river, a barn for raising silkworms, in the shelter of the woods, and a little church dedicated to St Agnes, at the intersection of the road to Vivier. Baldabiou hired thirty workers, brought a mysterious wooden machine from Italy, all wheels and gears, and said nothing more for seven months. Then he went back to the mayor and placed on his desk, in an orderly fashion, thirty thousand francs in large bills.

'Do you know what this is?'

'Money.'

'Wrong. It's the proof that you are an idiot.'

Then he picked up the bills, put them in his wallet, and turned to leave.

The mayor stopped him.

'What the devil should I do?'

'Nothing: and you will be the mayor of a wealthy town.'

Five years later Lavilledieu had seven silk mills and had become one of the principal centres in Europe for breeding silkworms and making silk. It wasn't all Baldabiou's property. Other prominent men and land-owners in the area had followed him in that curious entrepreneurial adventure. To each one, Baldabiou had revealed, without hesitation, the secrets of the work. This amused him much more than making piles of money. Teaching. And having secrets to tell. He was a man made like that.

7.

BALDABIOU was also the man who, eight years earlier, had changed Hervé Joncour's life. It was when the epidemics had first begun to hurt the European production of silk-worm eggs. Without getting upset, Baldabiou had studied the situation and had reached the conclusion that the problem would not be solved; it would be evaded. He had an idea; he lacked the right man. He realised he had found him when he saw Hervé Joncour passing by the café Verdun, elegant in the uniform of a second lieutenant of the infantry and with the proud bearing of a soldier on leave. He was twenty-four, at the time. Baldabiou invited him to his house, spread open before him an atlas full of exotic names, and said to him

'Congratulations. You've finally found a serious job, boy.'

Hervé Joncour listened to a long story about silk-worms, eggs, pyramids and travel by ship. Then he said

'I can't.'

'Why not?'

'In two days my leave is over – I have to return to Paris.'

'Military career?'

'Yes. It's what my father wanted.'

'No problem.'

He seized Hervé Joncour and led him to his father.

'You know who this is?' he asked, after entering the office unannounced.

'My son.'

'Look harder.'

The mayor sank back in his leather chair, beginning to sweat.

'My son Hervé, who in two days will return to Paris, where a brilliant career awaits him in our army, God and St Agnes willing.'

'Exactly. Only, God is busy elsewhere and St Agnes detests soldiers.'

A month later Hervé Joncour left for Egypt. He travelled on a ship called the *Adel*. In the cabins you could smell the odour of cooking, there was an Englishman who said he had fought at Waterloo, on the evening of the third day they saw dolphins sparkling on the horizon like drunken waves, at roulette it was always the sixteen.

He returned six months later – the first Sunday in

April, in time for High Mass – with thousands of eggs packed in cotton wool in two big wooden boxes. He had a lot of things to tell. But what Baldabiou said to him when they were alone was

  'Tell me about the dolphins.'

'The dolphins?'

'About when you saw them.'

That was Baldabiou.

No one knew how old he was.

8.

'*ALMOST* the entire world,' said Baldabiou softly. 'Almost', pouring a little water into his Pernod.

An August night, past twelve. Normally at that hour, Verdun had already been closed for a while. The chairs were turned upside down, neatly, on the tables. He had cleaned the bar, and all the rest. He had only to turn off the lights and lock up. But Verdun was waiting: Baldabiou was talking.

Sitting across from him, Hervé Joncour, with a spent cigarette between his lips, listened, unmoving. As he had eight years before, he was letting this man methodically rewrite his destiny. His voice came out thin and clear, punctuated by swallows of Pernod. He didn't stop for many minutes. The last thing he said was

'There is no choice. If we want to survive, we have to get there.'

Silence.

Verdun, leaning on the bar, looked over at the two of them.

Baldabiou was busy trying to find another drop of Pernod in the bottom of the glass.

Hervé Joncour placed the cigarette on the edge of the table before saying

'And where, exactly, might it be, this Japan?'

Baldabiou raised his walking stick and pointed it beyond the roofs of Saint-August.

'Straight that way.'

He said.

'At the end of the world.'

9.

IN those days Japan was, in effect, on the other side of the world. It was an island made up of islands, and for two hundred years had existed in complete isolation from the rest of humanity, rejecting any contact with the continent and prohibiting any foreigner from entering. The Chinese coast was almost two hundred miles distant, but an imperial decree had taken care to make it even farther, by forbidding throughout the island the construction of boats with more than one mast. Following a logic in its way enlightened, the law did not, however, prohibit emigration: but it condemned to death those who attempted to return. Chinese, Dutch and English traders had tried repeatedly to break through that absurd isolation, but they had been able only to set up a fragile and dangerous smuggling network. They had got little money, many troubles and some legends, good for selling in the ports, in the evening. Where they had failed, the Americans, thanks to the force of arms, succeeded. In July of 1853 Commodore Matthew C. Perry entered the bay of Yokohama with a fleet of modern steamships, and delivered to the Japanese an ultimatum in which he 'hoped for' the opening of the island to foreigners.

The Japanese had never before seen a ship capable of crossing the sea against the wind.

When, seven months later, Perry returned to receive the answer to his ultimatum, the military governor of the island yielded, signing an agreement in which he sanctioned the opening of two ports in the north of the island to foreigners, and the start of some modest commercial relations. From now on – the commodore declared with a certain solemnity – the sea around this island is not so deep.

10.

BALDABIOU knew all these stories. In particular he knew a legend that turned up repeatedly in the accounts of those who had been there. They said that that island produced the most beautiful silk in the world. It had been doing so for more than a thousand years, following rites and secrets that had achieved a mystic precision. What Baldabiou thought was that it was not a legend but the pure and simple truth. Once, he had held between his fingers a veil woven of Japanese silk thread. It was like holding between his fingers nothingness. So when everything seemed to be going to hell because of the pebrine and the infected eggs, what he thought was:

'That island is full of silkworms. And an island that no Chinese merchant or English insurer has managed to get to for two hundred years is an island that no infection will ever reach.'

He didn't confine himself to thinking this: he said it to all the silk producers of Lavilledieu, after calling them together at Verdun's café. None of them had ever heard talk of Japan.

'We should cross the whole world to buy healthy eggs in a place where when they see a foreigner they hang him?'

'Hanged him,' Baldabiou clarified.

They didn't know what to think. An objection occurred to some.

'There must be a reason that no one in the world has thought of going there to buy eggs.'

Baldabiou could bluff by reminding them that in the rest of the world there was no Baldabiou. But he preferred to say things as they were.

'The Japanese are resigned to selling their silk. But the eggs, no. They hold on to them tightly. And if you try to carry them off that island, what you do is a crime.'

The silk producers of Lavilledieu were – some more, some less – gentlemen, and would never have thought of breaking the law in their own country. The theory of doing so on the other side of the world, however, seemed to them eminently sensible.

II.

It was 1861. Flaubert was finishing *Salammbô*, electric light was still a hypothesis and Abraham Lincoln, on the other side of the ocean, was fighting a war whose end he would not see. The silkworm breeders of Lavilledieu joined together in a consortium and collected the considerable sum necessary for the expedition. To them all it seemed logical to entrust it to Hervé Joncour. When Baldabiou asked him to accept, he answered with a question.

'And where, exactly, might it be, this Japan?'

Straight that way. At the end of the world.

He left on October 6th. Alone.

At the gates of Lavilledieu he embraced his wife, Hélène, and said to her simply

'You mustn't be afraid of anything.'

She was a tall woman, she moved slowly, she had long black hair that she never gathered on to her head. She had a beautiful voice.

23

12.

HERVÉ Joncour left with eighty thousand francs in gold and the names of three men, obtained for him by Baldabiou: a Chinese, a Dutchman and a Japanese. He crossed the border near Metz, travelled through Württemberg and Bavaria, entered Austria, reached Vienna and Budapest by train, and continued to Kiev. On horseback he traversed two thousand kilometres of the Russian steppe, crossed the Urals into Siberia, and travelled for forty days to reach Lake Baikal, which the people of the place called: the sea. He followed the course of the River Amur, skirting the Chinese border, to the Ocean, and when he arrived at the Ocean he stopped in the port of Sabirk for eleven days, until a Dutch smugglers' ship carried him to Cape Teraya, on the western coast of Japan. On foot, taking secondary roads, he went through the provinces of Ishikawa, Toyama and Niigata, entered Fukushima, reached the city of Shirakawa, and rounded it on the east side; he waited two days for a man in black, who blindfolded him and led him to a village in the hills, where he spent one night, and the next morning he negotiated the purchase of the eggs with a man who didn't speak, and whose face was covered by a silk veil. Black. At sunset he hid the eggs in his bags, turned his back on Japan, and prepared to set off on the journey home.

He had just passed the last houses in the village when a man came running up, and stopped him. He said something in an agitated and peremptory tone, and led him back with polite insistence.

Hervé Joncour didn't speak Japanese, nor was he able to understand it, but he grasped that Hara Kei wanted to see him.

13.

A rice-paper panel slid open, and Hervé Joncour entered. Hara Kei was sitting cross-legged, on the floor, in the farthest corner of the room. He had on a dark tunic, and wore no jewels. The only visible sign of his power was a woman lying beside him, unmoving, her head resting on his lap, eyes closed, arms hidden under a loose red robe that spread around her, like a flame, on the ash-coloured mat. Slowly he ran one hand through her hair: he seemed to be caressing the coat of a precious, sleeping animal.

Hervé Joncour crossed the room, waited for a sign from his host, and sat down opposite him. A servant arrived, imperceptibly, and placed before them two cups of tea. Then he vanished. Hara Kei began to speak, in his own language, in a sing-song voice that melted into a sort of irritating artificial falsetto. Hervé Joncour listened. He kept his eyes fixed on those of Hara Kei and only for an instant, almost without realising it, lowered them to the face of the woman.

It was the face of a girl.

He raised them again.

Hara Kei paused, picked up one of the cups of tea, brought it to his lips, let some moments pass and said

'Try to tell me who you are.'

He said it in French, drawing out the vowels, in a hoarse voice but true.

14.

TO the most invincible man in Japan, the master of all that the world might take away from that island, Hervé Joncour tried to explain who he was. He did it in his own language, speaking slowly, without knowing precisely if Hara Kei was able to understand. Instinctively he rejected prudence, reporting simply, without inventions and without omissions, everything that was true. He set forth small details and crucial events in the same tone, and with barely visible gestures, imitating the hypnotic pace, melancholy and neutral, of a catalogue of objects rescued from a fire. Hara Kei listened, and not a shadow of an expression discomposed the features of his face. He kept his eyes fixed on Hervé Joncour's lips, as if they were the last lines of a farewell letter. The room was so silent and still that what happened unexpectedly seemed a huge event and yet was nothing.

Suddenly,

without moving at all,

that girl

opened her eyes.

Hervé Joncour did not pause but instinctively lowered his gaze to her, and what he saw, without pausing, was that those eyes *did not have an Oriental shape*, and that they were fixed, *with a disconcerting intensity*, on him: as if from the start, from under the eyelids, they had done nothing else. Hervé Joncour turned his gaze elsewhere, as naturally as he could, trying to continue his story with no perceptible difference in his voice. He stopped only when his eyes fell on the cup of tea, placed on the floor, in front of him. He took it in one hand, brought it to his lips, and drank slowly. He began to speak again as he set it down in front of him.

15.

FRANCE, the ocean voyages, the scent of the mulberry trees in Lavilledieu, the steam trains, Hélène's voice. Hervé Joncour continued to tell his story, as he had never in his life done. The girl continued to stare at him, with a violence that wrenched from every word the obligation to be memorable. The room seemed to have slipped into an irreversible stillness when suddenly, and in utter silence, she stuck one hand outside her robe and slid it along the mat in front of her. Hervé Joncour saw that pale spot reach the edge of his field of vision, saw it touch Hara Kei's cup of tea and then, absurdly, continue to slide until, without hesitation, it grasped the other cup, which was inexorably the cup *he* had drunk from, raised it lightly, and carried it away. Not for an instant had Hara Kei stopped staring expressionlessly at Hervé Joncour's lips.

The girl lifted her head slightly.

For the first time she took her eyes off Hervé Joncour and rested them on the cup.

Slowly, she rotated it until she had her lips at the exact point where he had drunk.

Half-closing her eyes, she took a sip of tea.

She removed the cup from her lips.

She slid it back to where she had picked it up.

Her hand vanished under her robe.

She rested her head again on Hara Kei's lap.

Eyes open, fixed on those of Hervé Joncour.

16.

HERVÉ Joncour spoke again at length. He stopped only when Hara Kei took his eyes off him and nodded his head slightly.

Silence.

In French, drawing out the vowels, in a hoarse voice but true, Hara Kei said

'If you are willing, I would like to see you return.'

For the first time he smiled.

'The eggs you have with you are fish eggs, worth little more than nothing.'

Hervé Joncour lowered his gaze. There was his cup of tea, in front of him. He picked it up and began to revolve it, and to observe it, as if he were searching for something on the painted line of the rim. When he found what he was looking for, he placed his lips there and drank. Then he put the cup down in front of him and said

'I know.'

Hara Kei laughed in amusement.

'Is that why you paid in false gold?'

'I paid for what I bought.'

Hara Kei became serious again.

'When you leave here you will have what you want.'

'When I leave this island, alive, you will receive the gold that is due you. You have my word.'

Hervé Joncour did not expect an answer. He rose, took a few steps backward, and bowed.

The last thing he saw, before he left, was her eyes, staring into his, perfectly mute.

17.

SIX days later Hervé Joncour embarked, at Takaoka, on a Dutch smugglers' ship, which took him to Sabirk. From there he went back along the Chinese border to Lake Baikal, journeyed over four thousand kilometres of Siberian territory, crossed the Urals, reached Kiev, and by train traversed all Europe, from east to west, until, after three months of travel, he arrived in France. On the first Sunday in April – in time for High Mass – he reached the gates of Lavilledieu. He stopped, thanked God, and entered the town on foot, counting his steps, so that each one should have a name, and so that he would never forget them.

'How is the end of the world?' asked Baldabiou.

'Invisible.'

For his wife, Hélène, he brought a silk tunic that she, out of modesty, never wore. If you held it between your fingers, it was like grasping nothing.

18.

THE eggs that Hervé Joncour brought from Japan – attached by the hundreds to little strips of mulberry bark – turned out to be perfectly healthy. The production of silk, in the region of Lavilledieu, was extraordinary that year, for quantity and for quality. Two more silk mills were opened, and Baldabiou had a cloister built beside the little church of St Agnes. It's not clear why, but he had imagined it round, so he entrusted the project to a Spanish architect named Juan Benitez, who enjoyed a certain notoriety in the field of *plazas de toros*.

'No sand in the middle, naturally, but a garden. And if possible dolphins' heads, in place of bulls', at the entrance.'

'Dolphins, *señor?*'

'Do you know the fish, Benitez?'

Hervé Joncour did the accounts twice and discovered that he was rich. He acquired thirty acres of land, south of his property, and spent the summer months designing a park where it would be pleasant to walk, and silent. He imagined it being invisible, like the end of the world. Every morning he went to Verdun's, where he listened to the news of the town and leafed through the papers that arrived from Paris. In the evenings he sat for a long time beside his wife, Hélène, beneath the portico of his house. She read a book, aloud, and this made him happy because he thought there was no voice more beautiful in the world.

He turned thirty-three on September 4, 1862. His life fell like rain before his eyes, a quiet spectacle.

19.

'YOU mustn't be afraid of anything.'

Since Baldabiou had made the decision, Hervé Joncour left for Japan on the first of October. He crossed the French border near Metz, travelled through Württemberg and Bavaria, entered Austria, reached Vienna and Budapest by train, and continued to Kiev. On horseback he traversed two thousand kilometres of the Russian steppe, crossed the Urals into Siberia, and travelled for forty days to reach Lake Baikal, which the people of the place called: the devil. He followed the course of the River Amur, skirting the Chinese border, to the Ocean, and when he arrived at the Ocean he stopped in the port of Sabirk for eleven days, until a Dutch smugglers' ship carried him to Cape Teraya, on the western coast of Japan. On foot, taking secondary roads, he went through the provinces of Ishikawa, Toyama and Niigata, entered Fukushima, reached the city of Shirakawa, and rounded it on the east side; he

39

waited two days for a man in black, who blindfolded him and led him to the village of Hara Kei. When he was able to open his eyes again, he found before him two servants, who took his bags and guided him to the edge of a wood, where they pointed out a path and left him alone. Hervé Joncour began walking in the shade that the trees, around and above him, carved out from the light of day. He stopped only when the foliage opened unexpectedly, for an instant, like a window, beside the path. A lake was visible, thirty yards below. And on the shore of the lake, squatting on the ground, with their backs to him, were Hara Kei and a woman in an orange robe, her hair loose on her shoulders. The instant Hervé Joncour saw her, she turned, slowly, for a moment, just long enough to meet his gaze.

Her eyes did not have an Oriental shape, and her face was the face of a girl.

Hervé Joncour began walking again, in the thick of the wood, and when he came out he was on the edge of the lake. A few steps ahead of him Hara Kei, alone, his back turned, sat motionless, dressed in black. Beside him was the orange robe, abandoned on the ground, and two straw sandals. Hervé Joncour approached. Tiny circular waves deposited the lake water on the shore, as if they had been sent there, from afar.

'My French friend,' murmured Hara Kei, without turning.

They spent hours, sitting beside one another, in talk and in silence. Then Hara Kei got up and Hervé Joncour followed him. With an imperceptible gesture, before setting off on the path Hervé Joncour let one of his gloves fall beside the orange robe, abandoned on the shore. It was already evening when they reached the town.

20.

HERVÉ Joncour remained the guest of Hara Kei for four days. It was like living at the court of a king. The whole town existed for him, and there was almost no action, in those hills, that was not carried out in his defence and for his pleasure. Life was seething in an undertone; it moved with a cunning languor, like a hunted animal in its den. The world seemed centuries away.

Hervé Joncour had a house for himself, and five servants who followed him everywhere. He ate alone, in the shade of a brightly flowering tree that he had never seen before. Twice a day they served him tea with a certain solemnity. In the evening, they accompanied him into the largest room of the house, which had a stone floor, and where the ritual of bathing was performed. Three old women, their faces covered by a sort of white greasepaint, ran the water over his body and dried him with warm silk cloths. Their hands were gnarled, but very light.

On the morning of the second day, Hervé Joncour saw a white man arrive in the town: accompanied by two carts filled with large wooden chests. He was English. He wasn't there to buy. He was there to sell.

'Weapons, *monsieur*. And you?'

'I am buying. Silkworms.'

They dined together. The Englishman had many stories to tell: he had been going back and forth between England and Japan for eight years. Hervé Joncour listened, and only at the end did he ask

'Do you know a woman, young, European I think, white, who lives here?'

The Englishman went on eating, impassive.

'White women do not exist in Japan. There is not a single white woman in Japan.'

He left the next day, loaded with gold.

21.

HERVÉ Joncour saw Hara Kei again only on the morning of the third day. He realised that the five servants had suddenly disappeared, as if by magic, and after a few moments Hara Kei arrived. The man for whom everyone, in that town, existed always moved within a bubble of emptiness. As if an unspoken rule had instructed the world to let him live alone.

Together they ascended the hillside, until they reached a clearing where the sky was streaked by the flight of dozens of birds with big blue wings.

'The people here watch them fly and in their flight they read the future.'

Said Hara Kei.

'When I was a boy my father brought me to a place like this, put his bow in my hands, and ordered me to shoot at one of them. I did, and a great bird, with blue wings, fell to earth, like a stone. Read the flight of your arrow if you want to know your future, my father said to me.'

The birds flew slowly, rising and falling in the sky, as if they wanted to erase it, very carefully, with their wings.

They returned to the town in the strange light of an afternoon that seemed evening. Arriving at the house of Hervé Joncour, they said goodbye. Hara Kei turned and began walking slowly, descending along the road that ran beside the river. Hervé Joncour stood on the threshold, watching him: he waited until he was some twenty paces away, then he said

'When will you tell me who that girl is?'

Hara Kei went on walking, with slow steps that bore no trace of weariness. Around him was the most absolute silence, and emptiness. As if by a special rule, wherever that man went, he went in an unconditional and perfect solitude.

22.

ON the morning of the last day, Hervé Joncour left his house and began to wander through the village. He met men who bowed at his passage and women who, lowering their gaze, smiled at him. He knew he had reached the dwelling of Hara Kei when he saw an immense aviary that held an incredible number of birds, of every type: a spectacle. Hara Kei had told him that he had had them brought from all corners of the earth. Some were worth more than all the silk that Lavilledieu could produce in a year. Hervé Joncour stopped to look at that magnificent folly. He recalled having read in a book that it was the custom for Oriental men to honour the faithfulness of their lovers by giving them not jewels but the most beautiful, elegant birds.

The dwelling of Hara Kei seemed to be drowning in a lake of silence. Hervé Joncour approached and stopped a few feet from the entrance. There were no doors, and on the paper walls shadows appeared and disappeared without a sound. It did not seem like life: if there was a name for all that, it was: theatre. Without knowing why, Hervé Joncour stopped to wait: he stood motionless, a few feet from the house. For the entire time that he conceded to destiny, that extraordinary stage let only shadows and silences filter through. So Hervé Joncour turned back, in the end, and began walking, quickly, towards his house. With his head bent, he stared at his steps, because this helped him not to think.

23.

THAT night Hervé Joncour packed his bags. Then he was led into the vast stone-floored room, for the ritual of bathing. He lay down, closed his eyes, and thought of the grand aviary, a mad token of love. A wet cloth was laid over his eyes. That had never been done before. Instinctively he began to remove it but a hand took his and stopped him. It was not the old hand of an old woman.

Hervé Joncour felt the water flow over his body, over his legs first, and then along his arms, and over his chest. Water like oil. And a strange silence, around him. He felt the lightness of a silk veil descend upon him. And the hands of a woman – of a woman – dried him, caressing his skin, everywhere: those hands, and that fabric woven of nothing. He never moved, not even when he felt the hands rise from his shoulders to his neck, and the fingers – the silk and the fingers – go to his lips, and touch them, once, slowly, and disappear.

Hervé Joncour felt the silk veil lifted up and removed. The last thing was a hand that opened his and placed something in the palm.

He waited for a long time, in the silence, without moving. Then slowly he took the damp cloth from his eyes. The room was almost dark. There was no one around. He got up, took the tunic that was lying folded on the floor, put it over his shoulders, left the room, went through the house, reached his mat, and lay down. He began to observe the tiny flame that quivered in the lantern. And, carefully, he stopped Time, for all the time that he desired.

It was nothing, then, to open his hand and look at the piece of paper. Small. A few ideograms drawn one under the other. Black ink.

24.

THE next day, early in the morning, Hervé Joncour left. Hidden in his baggage he carried thousands of silkworm eggs, that is, the future of Lavilledieu, and work for hundreds of people, and wealth for a tenth of them. Where the road curved to the left, hiding the view of the village forever behind the line of the hill, he stopped, paying no attention to the two men who accompanied him. He got off his horse and stood for a while beside the road, with his gaze fixed on those houses, climbing up the spine of the hill.

Six days later, Hervé Joncour embarked, at Takaoka, on a Dutch smugglers' ship, which took him to Sabirk. From there he went back along the Chinese border to Lake Baikal, journeyed over four thousand kilometres of Siberian territory, crossed the Urals, reached Kiev, and by train traversed all Europe, from east to west, until, after three months of travel, he arrived in France. The first Sunday of April – in time for High Mass – he reached the gates of Lavilledieu. He saw his wife, Hélène, running to meet him, and he smelled the perfume of her skin when he embraced her, and heard the velvet of her voice when she said to him

'You've returned.'

Tenderly.

'You've returned.'

25.

IN Lavilledieu life ran simply, regulated by a methodical normality. Hervé Joncour let it slide over him for forty-one days. On the forty-second he gave in, opened a drawer in his travel trunk, pulled out a map of Japan, unfolded it, and found the piece of paper he had hidden inside it, months before. A few ideograms drawn one under the other. Black ink. He sat at his desk, and examined them for a long time.

He found Baldabiou at Verdun's, playing billiards. He always played alone, against himself. Strange games. The normal man against the one-armed player, he called them. He made one shot in the usual way, and the next with one hand only. The day the one-armed player wins – he said – I will leave this city. For years, the one-armed player had been losing.

'Baldabiou, I have to find someone, here, who knows how to read Japanese.'

The one-armed player made a two-cushion draw shot.

'Ask Hervé Joncour, he knows everything.'

'I don't understand anything about it.'

'You're the Japanese, here.'

'But, just the same, I don't understand anything.'

The normal man leaned over his cue and made a follow shot for six points.

'Then there is only Madame Blanche. She has a fabric shop, in Nîmes. Above the shop is a bordello. That also belongs to her. She's wealthy. And she's Japanese.'

'Japanese? And how did she get here?'

'Don't ask if you want something from her. Shit.'

The one-armed player had just missed a three-cushion for fourteen points.

26.

To his wife, Hélène, Hervé Joncour said that he had to
go to Nîmes, on business. And that he would return the
same day.

He went up to the first floor, above the fabric shop,
at 12 Rue Moscat, and asked for Madame Blanche. He
was made to wait a long time. The parlour was decor-
ated as if for a party that had begun years earlier and
never ended. The girls were all young and French. There
was a pianist who, with a mute, played tunes that had
a Russian flavour. At the end of every piece he ran his
right hand through his hair and murmured softly

'*Voilà.*'

27.

HERVÉ Joncour waited for a couple of hours. Then he was led along the hallway, to the last door. He opened it and entered.

Madame Blanche was sitting in a large armchair, beside the window. She was wearing a kimono of a light material: completely white. On her fingers, as if they were rings, she wore little flowers of an intense blue. Shiny black hair, Oriental face, perfect.

'What makes you think you are rich enough to go to bed with me?'

Hervé Joncour remained standing, in front of her, with his hat in his hand.

'I need a favour from you. The price doesn't matter.'

Then he took from the inside pocket of his jacket a small piece of paper, folded in quarters, and held it out to her.

'I have to know what's written there.'

Madame Blanche didn't move an inch. Her lips were

slightly parted, they seemed the prehistory of a smile.

'I beg you, *madame*.'

She had no reason in the world to do it. And yet she took the piece of paper, unfolded it, looked at it. She raised her eyes to Hervé Joncour, lowered them. She folded the piece of paper, slowly. When she held it out, to give it back, the kimono fell open slightly, revealing her chest. Hervé Joncour saw that she had on nothing, underneath, and that her skin was young and white.

'Return, or I will die.'

She said it in a cold voice, looking Hervé Joncour in the eyes, and betraying not the least expression.

Return, or I will die.

Hervé Joncour put the piece of paper back in the inside pocket of his jacket.

'Thank you.'

He made a slight bow, then turned, went towards the door, and started to place some bills on the table.

'Forget about it.'

Hervé Joncour hesitated for a moment.

'I'm not talking about the money. I'm talking about that woman. Forget about it. She won't die and you know it.'

Without turning, Hervé Joncour placed the bills on the table, opened the door, and went out.

28.

BALDABIOU said that they came from Paris, sometimes, to make love with Madame Blanche. Returning to the capital, they displayed on the lapel of their evening jacket little blue flowers, the ones she always wore on her fingers, as if they were rings.

29.

THAT summer, for the first time in his life, Hervé Joncour took his wife to the Riviera. For two weeks they stayed in a hotel in Nice, frequented for the most part by English people and known for the musical evenings it offered its guests. Hélène was convinced that in a place so beautiful they would succeed in conceiving the child that they had expected, in vain, for years. Together they decided that it would be a boy. And that he would be named Philippe. In moderation they took part in the worldly life of the seaside resort, and enjoyed themselves later, in their room, laughing at the strange folk they had met. At a concert one evening, they met a fur dealer, a Pole: he said that he had been in Japan.

The night before they left, it happened that Hervé Joncour woke up, when it was still dark, and rose, and approached Hélène's bed. When she opened her eyes he heard his own voice saying softly:

'I will love you forever.'

30.

In early September the silkworm breeders of Lavilledieu met in order to decide what to do. The government had sent to Nîmes a young biologist whose mission was to study the disease that made the eggs produced in France useless. His name was Louis Pasteur: he worked with microscopes that could see the invisible: they said that he had already obtained extraordinary results. From Japan arrived news of an imminent civil war, stirred up by the forces opposed to foreigners entering the country. The French consulate, recently installed in Yokohama, sent dispatches that discouraged for the moment commercial relations with the island, suggesting that commerce should wait for better times. Inclined to prudence and sensitive to the costs that every clandestine expedition to Japan entailed, many of the leading men of Lavilledieu advanced the hypothesis that the journey of Hervé Joncour should be suspended that year and that they should trust to the shipments of eggs, mildly reliable, that came from the big importers in the Middle East. Baldabiou listened to them all, without saying a word. When at last it was his turn to speak, what he did was place his cane walking stick on the table and look at the man sitting opposite him. And wait.

Hervé Joncour knew of Pasteur's research and had read the news from Japan: but he had always refused to comment on it. He preferred to spend his time perfecting the plan for the park that he wanted to build around his house. Hidden in a corner of his study he kept a piece of paper folded in quarters, with a few ideograms drawn one on top of the other, black ink. He had a substantial sum in the bank, he led a peaceful life, and he had the reasonable illusion of soon becoming a father. When Baldabiou looked up at him what he said was

'You decide, Baldabiou.'

31.

HERVÉ Joncour left for Japan in early October. He crossed the French border near Metz, travelled through Württemberg and Bavaria, entered Austria, reached Vienna and Budapest by train, and continued to Kiev. On horseback he traversed two thousand kilometres of the Russian steppe, crossed the Urals into Siberia, and travelled for forty days to reach Lake Baikal, which the people of the place called: the last. He followed the course of the River Amur, skirting the Chinese border, to the Ocean, and when he arrived at the Ocean he stopped in the port of Sabirk for ten days, until a Dutch smugglers' ship carried him to Cape Teraya, on the western coast of Japan. What he found was a country in chaotic expectation of a war that wouldn't break out. He travelled for days without having to resort to his usual caution, since around him the map of power and the network of boundaries seemed to have dissolved in the imminence of an explosion that would totally remake them. At Shirakawa he met the man who was to take him to Hara Kei. In two days, on horseback, they came in sight of the village. Hervé Joncour entered on foot so that the news of his arrival could arrive before him.

32.

HE was led to one of the last houses in the village, high up, in the shelter of the wood. Five servants awaited him. He entrusted his baggage to them and went out on the veranda. At the opposite end of the village the house of Hara Kei was visible, not much bigger than the other houses, but surrounded by enormous cedars that protected its solitude. Hervé Joncour stood looking at it, as if nothing else existed, from there to the horizon. So he saw,

finally,

suddenly,

the sky above the house stained with the flight of hundreds of birds, as if they had exploded from the earth, birds of every type, astonished, fleeing everywhere, gone wild, singing and shouting, a pyrotechnic burst of wings, a cloud of colours shot into the light, of frightened sounds, music in flight, flying in the sky.

Hervé Joncour smiled.

33.

THE village started swarming like a crazed anthill: everyone ran and shouted, looking up and pursuing the fugitive birds, for years the pride of their Lord, and now a flying mockery in the sky. Hervé Joncour came out of his house and walked down through the village, slowly, gazing straight ahead with infinite calm. No one seemed to see him, and he seemed to see nothing. He was a thread of gold running straight into the woof of a carpet woven by a madman. He crossed the bridge over the river, descended to the great cedars, entered their shade and emerged from it. Facing him was the enormous aviary, with the doors wide open, completely empty. And in front of it a woman. Hervé Joncour didn't look around, he continued simply to walk, slowly, and he stopped only when he was before her.

Her eyes didn't have an Oriental shape and her face was the face of a girl.

Hervé Joncour took a step towards her, reached out

a hand and opened it. In the palm was a small sheet of paper, folded in quarters. She saw it and every corner of her face smiled. She placed her hand in Hervé Joncour's, she pressed it gently, hesitated a moment, then withdrew it, clutching that piece of paper which had gone around the world. She had just hidden it in a fold of her dress, when the voice of Hara Kei was heard.

'Welcome, my French friend.'

He was a few steps away. His kimono dark, black hair gathered, in perfect order, at the nape. He approached. He began to examine the aviary, looking at the open doors, one by one.

'They'll come back. It's always difficult to resist the temptation to come back, isn't that true?'

Hervé Joncour didn't answer. Hara Kei looked him in the eyes and said softly

'Come.'

Hervé Joncour followed him. He took some steps, and then turned towards the girl and made a slight bow.

'I hope to see you again soon.'

Hara Kei continued to walk.

'She doesn't know your language.'

He said.

'Come.'

34.

THAT evening Hara Kei invited Hervé Joncour to his house. There were men from the village and elegantly dressed women, their faces painted in garish colours and white. They drank sake and, in long wooden pipes, smoked tobacco with a bitter and stupefying aroma. Jugglers arrived and a man who got laughs by imitating men and animals. Three old women played stringed instruments, with never a break in their smiles. Hara Kei was sitting in the place of honour, wearing dark robes, his feet bare. In a splendid silk dress the woman with the face of a girl sat beside him. Hervé Joncour was at the extreme opposite end of the room: he was assaulted by the cloying perfume of the women around him, and he smiled in embarrassment at the men, who amused themselves by telling him stories he couldn't understand. A thousand times he searched for her eyes and a thousand times she found his. It was a kind of sad dance, secret and impotent. Hervé Joncour danced late into the night, then he rose, said some words in French to excuse himself, somehow got free of a woman who had decided to accompany him, and, making his way amid clouds of smoke and men who addressed him in their incomprehensible language, he went out. Before leaving the room, he looked at her a last time. She was looking at him, eyes perfectly mute, centuries distant.

Hervé Joncour wandered through the village breathing the cool night air and getting lost in the alleys that climbed the hillside. When he reached his house he saw a lantern, lighted, swaying behind the paper walls. He entered and found two women standing before him. An Oriental girl, young, dressed in a simple white kimono. And her. She had in her eyes a kind of feverish joy. She didn't leave him time to do anything. She approached, took one hand, brought it to her face, touched it with her lips, and then, holding it tight, placed it on the hands of the girl who was beside her, and held it there, so that it couldn't escape. She removed her hand, finally, took two steps back, picked up the lantern, looked for an instant into the eyes of Hervé Joncour, and ran off. It was an orange lantern. It disappeared into the night, a tiny light in flight.

35.

HERVÉ Joncour had never seen that girl, nor, really, did he ever see her, that night. In the room without lights he felt the beauty of her body, and knew her hands and her mouth. He loved her for hours, with gestures that he had never made, letting himself be taught a slowness that he didn't know. In the dark, it was nothing to love her and not to love her.

A little before dawn, the girl rose, put on the white kimono, and left.

36.

In the morning, Hervé Joncour found a man from Hara Kei waiting for him, across from his house. He had with him fifteen sheets of mulberry bark, completely covered with eggs: tiny, ivory-coloured. Hervé Joncour examined each sheet, carefully, then negotiated the price and paid in gold scales. Before the man left he made him understand that he wished to see Hara Kei. The man shook his head. Hervé Joncour understood, from his gestures, that Hara Kei had left that morning, early, with his entourage, and no one knew when he would return.

Hervé Joncour went through the village quickly, to the dwelling of Hara Kei. He found only some servants, who responded to every question by shaking their heads. The house seemed deserted. And although he looked carefully all around, even at the most insignificant things, he saw nothing resembling a message for him. He left the house and, returning to the village, passed the immense aviary. The doors were closed again. Inside, hundreds of birds were flying, sheltered from the sky.

37.

HERVÉ Joncour waited two more days for some sign. Then he left.

It happened that, no more than half an hour from the village, he passed a wood from which came a singular, silvery din. Hidden among the leaves he could make out the thousand dark patches of a flock of birds that were still and at rest. With no explanation to the two men who accompanied him, Hervé Joncour stopped his horse, took the revolver from his belt, and fired six shots into the air. The birds, terrorised, rose into the sky, like a cloud of smoke released by a fire. It was so big that you could have seen it days' and days' walk from there. Dark in the sky, with no other purpose than its own bewilderment.

38.

Six days later Hervé Joncour embarked, at Takaoka, on a Dutch smugglers' ship, which took him to Sabirk. From there he went back along the Chinese border to Lake Baikal, journeyed over four thousand kilometres of Siberian territory, crossed the Urals, reached Kiev, and by train traversed all Europe, from east to west, until, after three months of travel, he arrived in France. The first Sunday in April – in time for High Mass – he reached the gates of Lavilledieu. He halted the carriage, and for some minutes sat without moving behind the drawn curtains. Then he got out, and continued on foot, step after step, with infinite weariness.

Baldabiou asked him if he had seen the war.

'Not the one I expected,' he answered.

At night he went to Hélène's bed and loved her so impatiently that she was frightened and couldn't hold back her tears. When he noticed, she forced herself to smile at him.

'It's just that I'm so happy,' she said softly.

39.

HERVÉ Joncour delivered the eggs to the silkworm breeders of Lavilledieu. Then, for days, he did not appear again in the town, neglecting even his usual daily outing to Verdun's. In early May, to general amazement, he bought the house abandoned by Jean Berbeck, the man who had stopped speaking one day and had not said another word for the rest of his life. Everyone thought that he intended to make it his new workshop. He didn't even start to clear it out. He would go there, from time to time, and remain in those rooms alone, doing what, no one knew. One day he took Baldabiou there.

'Do you know why Jean Berbeck stopped speaking?' Baldabiou asked.

'It's one of the many things he never said.'

Years had passed, but there were still paintings hanging on the walls and dishes in the drain, beside the sink. It wasn't a happy sight, and Baldabiou, on his own, would willingly have left. But Hervé Joncour continued to look with fascination at those dead, mouldy walls. It was obvious: he was looking for something in there.

'Maybe it's that life, at times, gets to you in a way that there's really nothing more to say.'

He said.

'Nothing more, forever.'

Baldabiou wasn't much cut out for serious conversations. He was staring at Jean Berbeck's bed.

'Maybe anyone would become mute in such a hideous house.'

For days Hervé Joncour continued to lead a retired life; he was hardly seen in the town, and spent his time working on the plan for the park that sooner or later he would build. He filled sheets and sheets with strange designs that looked like machines. One evening Hélène asked him

'What is it?'

'It's an aviary.'

'An aviary?'

'Yes.'

'And what is its purpose?'

Hervé Joncour kept his eyes fixed on those drawings.

'You fill it with birds, as many as you can, then one day, when something lovely happens to you, you open the doors and watch them fly away.'

40.

AT the end of July Hervé Joncour left, with his wife, for Nice. They settled themselves in a small villa, on the sea. That was what Hélène had wanted, convinced that a serene and quiet retreat would soothe the melancholy humour that seemed to have possessed her husband. She had had the acuity, nonetheless, to pass it off as a personal whim, giving the man she loved the pleasure of indulging her.

They spent five weeks of small-scale, unassailable happiness. On days when the heat was less intense, they rented a carriage and enjoyed discovering the towns hidden in the hills, where the sea seemed a background of coloured paper. From time to time, they went to the city for a concert or some society event. One evening they accepted the invitation of an Italian baron who was celebrating his sixtieth birthday with a grand dinner at the Hôtel Suisse. They were at dessert when Hervé Joncour happened to look over at Hélène. She was sitting on the other side of the table, beside a seductive Englishman who, curiously, displayed on the lapel of his evening suit a little wreath of small blue flowers. Hervé Joncour saw him lean over Hélène and whisper something in her ear. Hélène began to laugh, in a beautiful way, and, laughing, bent slightly towards the English gentleman so that she grazed his shoulder with her hair, in a gesture in which there was nothing embarrassing but only a disconcerting precision. Hervé Joncour lowered his gaze to his plate. He couldn't help noticing that his own hand, clutching a silver teaspoon, was undeniably trembling.

Later, in the smoking room, Hervé Joncour, staggering because he had drunk too much, approached a man who, sitting alone at the table, was looking straight ahead, with a vaguely doltish expression on his face. He leaned over towards him and said slowly

'I must communicate to you something very important, *monsieur*. We are all revolting. We are all marvellous, and we are all revolting.'

The man came from Dresden. He dealt in calves and didn't understand much French. He burst into a noisy laugh, making a sign of agreement with his head, repeatedly: as if he would never stop.

Hervé Joncour and his wife stayed on the Riviera

until early September. They left the little villa with regret, since, within its walls, they had felt that to love each other was an easy fate.

41.

BALDABIOU arrived at the house of Hervé Joncour early in the morning. They sat under the portico.

'As a park it's not much.'

'I haven't started to build it yet, Baldabiou.'

'Ah, I see.'

Baldabiou never smoked in the morning. He took out his pipe, filled it, and lighted it.

'I met this Pasteur. He's a smart fellow. He showed me what he's doing. He's capable of distinguishing the sick eggs from the healthy ones. He doesn't know how to cure them, of course. But he can isolate the healthy ones. And he says that probably thirty per cent of what we produce is healthy.'

Pause.

'They say that war has broken out in Japan, this time for real. The English give arms to the government, the Dutch to the rebels. The two seem to be in agreement. They incite them to explode and then they take everything and divide it. The French consulate looks on, those people are always looking on. All they're good for is sending dispatches that tell of massacres, of foreigners slaughtered like sheep.'

Pause.

'Is there any more coffee?'

Hervé Joncour poured some coffee.

Pause.

'Those two Italians, Ferreri and the other, the ones who went to China, last year . . . They came back with fifteen thousand ounces of eggs, good stuff, and they also bought from Bollet, it's said the stock was high quality. In a month they leave again . . . They offered a good deal, their prices are honest, eleven francs an ounce, all covered by insurance. They are serious people, with an organisation behind them – they sell eggs to half of Europe. Serious people, I tell you.'

Pause.

'I don't know. Perhaps we could manage. With our eggs, with the work of Pasteur, and then what we can buy from the two Italians . . . we could manage. The others in town say it's madness to send you out there again . . . with all that it costs . . . they say it's too risky, and in this they are right, the other times it was different, but now . . . now it's difficult to get back from there alive.'

Pause.

'The fact is that they don't want to lose the eggs. And I don't want to lose you.'

Hervé Joncour sat for a while gazing at the park that wasn't there. Then he did something he had never done.

'I will go to Japan, Baldabiou.'

He said.

'I will buy those eggs, and if necessary I'll do it with my own money. You must only decide if I sell them to you or to someone else.'

Baldabiou hadn't expected this. It was like seeing the one-armed man win on the last play, four cushions, impossible angles.

42.

BALDABIOU told the breeders of Lavilledieu that Pasteur was undependable, that those Italians had already scammed half of Europe, that in Japan the war would end before winter, and that St Agnes, in a dream, had asked him if they weren't a pack of chickenshits. Only to Hélène he couldn't lie.

'Is it really necessary for him to go, Baldabiou?'

'No.'

'Then why?'

'I can't stop him. And if he wants to go, I can only give him one more reason to return.'

All the breeders of Lavilledieu contributed, although reluctantly, their quota to finance the expedition. Hervé Joncour began his preparations, and in early October he was ready to leave. Hélène, as she did every year, helped him, without asking questions, and hiding from him any worry she had. Only the last night, after turning off the lamp, did she find the strength to say to him

'Promise me that you will return.'

In a firm voice, without tenderness.

'Promise me that you will return.'

In the darkness Hervé Joncour answered

'I promise.'

43.

ON October 10, 1864, Hervé Joncour left on his fourth
trip to Japan. He crossed the French border near Metz,
travelled through Württemberg and Bavaria, entered
Austria, reached Vienna and Budapest by train, and
continued to Kiev. On horseback he traversed two thousand kilometres of the Russian steppe, crossed the Urals
into Siberia, and travelled for forty days to reach Lake
Baikal, which the people of the place called: the saint.
He followed the course of the River Amur, skirting the
Chinese border, to the Ocean, and when he arrived at
the Ocean he stopped in the port of Sabirk for eight
days, until a Dutch smugglers' ship carried him to Cape
Teraya, on the western coast of Japan. On horseback,
taking secondary roads, he crossed the provinces of
Ishikawa, Toyama, Niigata, and entered Fukushima.
When he reached Shirakawa he found the city half
destroyed, and a garrison of government soldiers
camped among the ruins. He circled the city to the east,

and waited for the emissary from Hara Kei for five days, in vain. At dawn on the sixth day he left for the hills, to the north. He had a few rough maps, and what was left of his memories. He wandered for days, until he recognised a river, and then a forest, and then a road. At the end of the road he found the village of Hara Kei: burned to the ground – houses, trees, everything.

There was nothing.

Not a living soul.

Hervé Joncour stood motionless, looking at the enormous spent brazier. Behind him was a road eight thousand kilometres long. And in front of him nothing. Suddenly he saw what he had thought was invisible.

The end of the world.

44.

HERVÉ Joncour stayed for hours among the ruins of the village. He couldn't leave, although he knew that every hour lost there could signify disaster for him, and for all Lavilledieu: he had no silkworm eggs, and even if he had found some he had only a couple of months to get across the world before they would hatch, on the way, becoming a mass of useless larvae. So he stayed there until something surprising and irrational happened: suddenly, out of nowhere, a boy appeared. Dressed in rags, he walked slowly, staring at the stranger with fear in his eyes. Hervé Joncour didn't move. The boy took a few more steps and stopped. They stood looking at each other, a few feet apart. Then the boy took something from under the rags and, trembling with fear, approached Hervé Joncour and held it out to him. A glove. Hervé Joncour saw again the edge of a lake, and an orange robe abandoned on the ground, and the small waves that pushed the water on to the shore, as if sent there from afar. He took the glove and smiled at the boy.

'It's me, the Frenchman . . . the silk man, the Frenchman, do you understand? . . . It's me.'

The boy stopped trembling.

'French . . .'

His eyes were bright, but he laughed. He began to speak, quickly, almost shouting, and running, making a sign to Hervé Joncour to follow him. He disappeared on a path into the woods, in the direction of the mountains.

Hervé Joncour didn't move. He turned the glove over and over in his hands, as if it were the only thing left to him of a vanished world. He knew that by now it was too late. And that he had no choice.

He rose. Slowly he approached his horse. He got in the saddle. Then he did a strange thing. He pressed his heels into the animal's belly. And set off. Towards the forest, behind the boy, beyond the end of the world.

45.

THEY travelled for days, northward, in the mountains. Hervé Joncour didn't know where they were going: but he let the boy guide him, without attempting to ask. They came across two villages. The people hid in their houses. The women ran away. The boy vastly amused himself by shouting at them incomprehensibly. He was no more than fourteen. He was constantly blowing on a small reed instrument, from which he drew forth the songs of all the birds in the world. He appeared to be doing the most wonderful thing in his life.

On the fifth day they reached the top of a hill. The boy indicated a point on the road in front of them, which descended to a valley. Hervé Joncour took the telescope and what he saw was a kind of procession: armed men, women and children, carts, animals. An entire village: on the road. Hervé Joncour saw Hara Kei, on horseback, dressed in black. Behind him, enclosed on all four sides by bright-coloured fabrics, was a litter, swaying.

46.

THE boy got off the horse, said something, and ran away. Before disappearing among the trees he turned and stood there for a moment, searching for a gesture to indicate that it had been a wonderful journey.

'It's been a wonderful journey,' Hervé Joncour called out to him.

All day, at a distance, Hervé Joncour followed the caravan. When he saw it stop for the night, he continued along the road until two armed men came up to him and took his horse and his bags and led him to a tent. He waited for a long time, then Hara Kei arrived. He made no sign of greeting. He didn't even sit down.

'How did you get here, Frenchman?'

Hervé Joncour didn't answer.

'I asked who brought you here.'

Silence.

'There is nothing for you here. There is only war. And it's not your war. Go away.'

Hervé Joncour took out a small leather purse, opened it, and emptied it on the ground. Scales of gold.

'War is an expensive game. You need me. I need you.'

Hara Kei didn't even look at the gold on the ground. He turned and left.

47.

HERVÉ Joncour spent the night on the edge of the camp. No one spoke to him, no one seemed to see him. They all slept on the ground, beside fires. There were only two tents. Next to one, Hervé Joncour saw the litter, empty: hanging on the four corners were some small cages: birds. From the mesh of the cages hung tiny gold bells. They jingled, softly, in the night breeze.

48.

WHEN he woke, he saw that the village was about to set off again. The tents were gone. The litter was still there, open. The people climbed on to the carts, silently. He got up and looked around for a long time, but only eyes of an Oriental shape met his, and were immediately lowered. He saw armed men and children who didn't cry. He saw the mute faces that people have when they are a people in flight. And he saw a tree, on the side of the road. And suspended from a branch the boy who had brought him there, hanged.

Hervé Joncour approached and stood staring for a moment, as if hypnotised. Then he untied the rope that was attached to the tree, picked up the boy's body, laid it on the ground, and knelt beside it. He couldn't take his eyes from that face. So he didn't see the village starting off, but only heard, as if from a distance, the noise of the procession as it brushed past him, along the road. He didn't look up even when he heard the voice of Hara Kei, a step away, saying

'Japan is an ancient country, do you understand? Its law is ancient: there are twelve crimes for which a man can be condemned to death. And one is to carry a message of love from one's mistress.'

Hervé Joncour didn't take his eyes off that murdered boy.

'He had no message of love with him.'

'He *was* a message of love.'

Hervé Joncour felt something pressing on his head, forcing it towards the ground.

'It's a gun, Frenchman. Don't look up, I beg you.'

Hervé Joncour didn't understand immediately. Then, amid the rustling sounds of that caravan in flight, he heard the gilded tinkle of a thousand tiny bells approaching, gradually, ascending the road towards him, step by step, and although in his eyes there was only that dark earth, he could imagine the litter, swaying like a pendulum, and almost see it, ascending, foot after foot, approaching, slow but implacable, borne by that sound which grew louder and louder, intolerably loud, closer and closer, so close that it touched him, a gilded din, right in front of him now, precisely in front of him – at that moment – that woman – in front of him.

Hervé Joncour raised his head.

Marvellous fabrics, silk, draping the litter, a thousand colours, orange, white, ochre, silver, not a peephole in that marvellous nest, only the rustling of the colours rippling in the air, impenetrable, lighter than nothing.

Hervé Joncour didn't hear an explosion shatter its life. He heard the sound growing distant, the barrel of the rifle lifted up and the voice of Hara Kei saying softly

'Go away, Frenchman. And don't ever come back.'

49.

ONLY silence, along the road. The body of a boy, on the ground. A man kneeling. Until the last light of day.

50.

IT took Hervé Joncour eleven days to reach Yokohama. He bribed a Japanese official and procured sixteen cartons of silkworm eggs that came from the south of the island. He wrapped them in silk cloths and sealed them in four round wooden boxes. He found a ship for the continent and in early March reached the Russian coast. He chose the northernmost route, looking for cold to arrest the life of the eggs and prolong the time before they hatched. By forced marches he covered the four thousand kilometres of Siberia, crossed the Urals, and reached St Petersburg. He bought, at an exorbitant cost, hundredweights of ice and loaded them, with the eggs, into the hold of a merchant ship bound for Hamburg. It took six days to get there. He unloaded the four round wooden boxes, and got a train heading south. After eleven hours of travel, just outside a city that was called Eberfeld, the train stopped to take on water. Hervé Joncour looked around. A summer sun was beating on the fields of grain, and on all the world. Sitting opposite him was a Russian merchant: he had taken off his shoes and was fanning the air with the last page of a newspaper written in German. Hervé Joncour stared at him. He saw the stains of sweat on his shirt and the drops that pearled his forehead and neck. The Russian said something, laughing. Hervé Joncour smiled at him, rose, took his bags, and got off the train. He walked beside it to the last car, a freight car that carried fish and meat, preserved in ice. It was dripping water like a bowl punctured by a thousand projectiles. He opened the door, climbed into the car, and, one after another, picked up his round wooden boxes, carried them outside, and set them on the ground, beside the tracks. Then he closed the door and waited. When the train was ready to leave they shouted to him to hurry and get on. He responded by shaking his head, and making a gesture of farewell. He saw the train grow distant, and then disappear. He waited until he no longer heard it. Then he bent over one of the wooden boxes, removed the seals, and opened it. He did the same with the three others. Slowly, with care.

Millions of larvae. Dead.

It was May 6, 1865.

51.

HERVÉ Joncour entered Lavilledieu nine days later. From a distance, his wife, Hélène, saw the carriage coming along the tree-lined drive of the villa. She said to herself that she mustn't weep and that she mustn't flee.

She went to the front door, opened it, and stopped on the threshold.

When Hervé Joncour came close to her, she smiled. He, embracing her, said softly

'Stay with me, please.'

They were awake late into the night, sitting beside each other on the lawn in front of the house. Hélène told him about Lavilledieu, and all those months spent waiting, and of the past days, terrible.

'You were dead.'

She said.

'And there was nothing good left, in the world.'

52.

AROUND the farmhouses, in Lavilledieu, people looked at the mulberries, thick with leaves, and saw their own ruin. Baldabiou had found some shipments of eggs, but the larvae died as soon as they emerged. The rough silk that was obtained from the few that survived was barely enough to provide work for two of the seven silk mills in the town.

'Do you have any ideas?' asked Baldabiou.

'One,' answered Hervé Joncour.

The next day he let it be known that, in the summer months, he would build the park for his villa. He engaged men and women, in the town, by the dozens. They deforested the hill and rounded its contours, making the slope that led to the valley gentler. With trees and hedges they designed delicate, transparent labyrinths on the earth. With flowers of every kind they built gardens that appeared by surprise, like clearings, in the heart of small birch woods. They diverted water from the river, so that it would descend, from fountain to fountain, to the western edge of the park, where it pooled in a small lake, surrounded by meadows. To the south, amid lemon and olive trees, they built a large aviary, of wood and iron: it looked like a piece of embroidery suspended in the air.

They worked for four months. At the end of September the park was ready. No one, in Lavilledieu, had ever seen anything like it. They said that Hervé Joncour had spent all his capital. They said, too, that he had returned from Japan changed, perhaps ill. They said that he had sold the eggs to the Italians and now had a patrimony in gold that was waiting for him in the banks of Paris. They said that if it were not for the park they would have died of hunger, that year. They said that he was a swindler. They said that he was a saint. Someone said: something is troubling him, some kind of unhappiness.

53.

ALL that Hervé Joncour said about his journey was that the eggs had hatched in a town near Cologne, and that the town was called Eberfeld.

Four months and thirteen days after his return, Baldabiou sat before him, on the shore of the lake, on the western edge of the park, and said

'After all, sooner or later, you'll have to tell someone the truth.'

He said it softly, because he didn't believe, ever, that the truth was good for anything.

It was autumn and the light, around them, was unnatural.

'The first time I saw Hara Kei he was wearing a dark tunic, and he was sitting motionless, with his legs crossed, in the corner of a room. Lying beside him, her head resting on his lap, was a woman. Her eyes didn't have an Oriental shape, and her face was the face of a girl.'

Baldabiou listened in silence, until the end, until the train at Eberfeld.

He didn't think anything.

He listened.

It hurt him to hear, finally, Hervé Joncour say softly

'I never even heard her voice.'

And after a while:

'It's a strange grief.'

Softly.

'To die of nostalgia for something you will never live.'

They went back across the park walking one beside the other. The only thing Baldabiou said was

'Why the hell is it so damn cold?'

He said it at a certain point.

54.

At the start of the new year – 1866 – Japan legalised the export of silkworm eggs.

In the following decade France alone would import ten million francs' worth of Japanese eggs.

Furthermore, starting in 1869, with the opening of the Suez Canal, the journey to Japan took no more than twenty days. And just under twenty days for the return.

Artificial silk was patented, in 1884, by a Frenchman named Chardonnet.

55.

Six months after his return to Lavilledieu, Hervé Joncour received in the post a mustard-coloured envelope. When he opened it, he found inside seven sheets of paper, covered by a thick geometric writing: black ink: Japanese ideograms. Apart from the name and the address on the envelope, there was not a single word written in Western characters. From the stamps, the letter seemed to have come from Ostend.

Hervé Joncour unfolded it and examined it for a long time. It seemed a catalogue of little bird tracks, compiled with meticulous folly. It was surprising to think that in fact they were signs; that is, the ashes of an incinerated voice.

56.

FOR days and days Hervé Joncour kept the letter with him, folded in two, in his pocket. If he changed his clothes, he moved it into the new ones. He never opened it to look. Every so often he turned it over in his hands, while he was talking with a farmer, or sitting on the veranda waiting till it was time for dinner. One evening he began to examine it against the light of the lamp, in his study. In transparency, the tiny bird tracks spoke in a blurred voice. They said something absolutely insignificant or something that could unhinge a life: it wasn't possible to know, and this Hervé Joncour liked. He heard Hélène coming. He placed the letter on the table. She came in and, as she did every night, before retiring to her room, kissed him. When she leaned over him, her nightgown fell open slightly, revealing her chest. Hervé Joncour saw that she had nothing on, underneath, and that her breasts were small and white like those of a girl.

For four days he went on with his life, with no change in his prudent daily rituals. On the morning of the fifth day he put on a fine grey suit and left for Nîmes. He said that he would return before evening.

57.

AT 12 Rue Moscat, everything was the same as three years before. The celebration was not yet over. The girls were all young and French. The pianist played, with the mute, themes that had a Russian flavour. Perhaps it was old age, perhaps some vile grief: at the end of each number he no longer ran his right hand through his hair and murmured, softly,

'*Voilà.*'

He was silent, looking at his hands in dismay.

58.

MADAME Blanche received him without a word. Her hair black, lustrous, her face Oriental, perfect. Little blue flowers on her fingers, as if they were rings. A long, almost transparent white robe. Bare feet.

Hervé Joncour sat down opposite her. He took a letter out of his pocket.

'Do you remember me?'

Madame Blanche nodded, with an infinitesimal movement of her head.

'I need you again.'

He held out the letter. She had no reason to do it, but she took it and opened it. She examined the seven sheets, one by one, then looked up at Hervé Joncour.

'I don't love this language, *monsieur*. I wish to forget it, and I wish to forget that land, and my life there, and everything.'

Hervé Joncour sat immobile, his hands gripping the arms of his chair.

'I will read this letter for you. I will do it. And I don't want money. But I want a promise: don't ever come back and ask this again.'

'I promise, *madame*.'

She stared into his eyes. Then she lowered her gaze to the first page of the letter, rice paper, black ink.

'*My beloved lord*'

she said

'*don't be afraid, don't move, be silent, no one will see us.*'

59.

Stay like that, I want to look at you, I looked at you so much but you weren't for me, now you are mine, don't come near me, please, stay as you are, we have one night for us, and I want to look at you, I've never seen you like that, your body mine, your skin, close your eyes, and caress yourself, please

Said Madame Blanche, Hervé Joncour listened,

don't open your eyes if you can, and caress yourself, your hands are beautiful, I've dreamed of them so many times now I want to see them, I like seeing them on your skin, like that, please go on, don't open your eyes, I'm here, no one can see us and I am near you, caress yourself my beloved lord, caress your sex, please, gently,

she stopped, 'Continue, please', he said,

*your hand on your sex is beautiful, don't stop, I like
watching it and watching you, my beloved lord, don't
open your eyes, not yet, you mustn't be afraid, I'm near
you, do you hear me? I'm here, I can touch you, this is
silk, do you feel it? It's the silk of my robe, don't open
your eyes and you will have my skin,*

she said, she read softly, with the voice of a child-
woman,

*you will have my lips, when I touch you for the first time
it will be with my lips, you won't know where, at some
point you will feel the warmth of my lips, on you, you
can't know where if you don't open your eyes, don't open
them, somewhere you'll feel my mouth, suddenly,*

he listened without moving, from the pocket of his grey
suit a bright white handkerchief stuck out,

*maybe it will be your eyes, I will rest my mouth on
your eyelids and eyebrows, you will feel the warmth go
into your head, and my lips on your eyes, inside, or
maybe it will be your sex, I'll place my lips there, and,
opening them, descend, little by little,*

she said, her head was bent over the pages, and one hand brushed her neck, slowly,

I will let your sex half close my mouth, entering between my lips, pressing my tongue, and my saliva will run along your skin to your hand, my kiss and your hand, one inside the other, on your sex,

he listened, he kept his gaze fixed on an empty silver frame, hanging on the wall,

until finally I will kiss your heart, because I want you, I will bite the skin that beats over your heart, because I want you, and with your heart in my mouth you'll be mine, truly, with my mouth in your heart you'll be mine, forever, if you don't believe me open your eyes my beloved lord and look at me, it's me, who can ever cancel out this moment that's happening, and this my body now without silk, your hands touching it, your eyes looking at it,

she said, she was leaning towards the lamp, the light struck the pages and went through her transparent robe, *your fingers in my sex, your tongue on my lips, you who slide under me, hold my hips, pick me up, let me slide over your sex, slowly, who can destroy this, you inside me moving slowly, your hands on my face, your fingers in my mouth, the pleasure in your eyes, your voice, you move slowly but until you hurt me, my pleasure, my voice,*

he listened, at a certain point he turned to look at her, he saw her, he wanted to lower his eyes but couldn't,

my body on yours, your back that raises me up, your arms that won't let me go, the thrusting inside me, it's a sweet violence, I see your eyes searching mine, they want to know how far to hurt me, as far as you want, my beloved, there is no end, it will not end, do you see? No one will be able to destroy this moment that is happening, forever you will throw your head back, crying, forever I will close my eyes wiping the tears from my brow, my voice in yours, your violence holding me tight, there is no longer time to flee or force to resist, it was to be this moment, and is this moment, believe me, my beloved, will be this moment, from now on, will be until the end, she said, in a whisper, then she stopped.

There were no other marks on the page that she had in her hand: the last. But when she turned it over to put it down she saw on the back some more orderly lines, black ink in the centre of the white page. She looked up at Hervé Joncour. His eyes were fixed on her, and she realised that they were beautiful eyes. She lowered her gaze to the page.

We will not see each other anymore, my lord.

She said.

What there was for us we have done, and you know it. Believe me: we have done it forever. Keep your life safe from me. And don't hesitate for a moment, if it is useful for your happiness, to forget this woman who now, without regret, says farewell.

She remained looking at the page for a while, then placed it on the others, beside her, on a small pale-wood table. Hervé Joncour didn't move. Only he turned his head and lowered his eyes. He was staring at the crease in his trousers, barely perceptible but perfect, on the right leg, from the groin to the knee, imperturbable.

Madame Blanche rose, bent over the lamp, and turned it off. A faint light came in through the window, from the parlour. She went over to Hervé Joncour, took from her fingers a ring of tiny blue flowers, and laid it beside him. Then she crossed the room, opened a small painted door hidden in the wall, and disappeared, half-closing it behind her.

Hervé Joncour sat for a long time in that strange light, turning over and over in his fingers a ring of tiny blue flowers. Weary notes from a piano reached him from the parlour: they were losing time, so that you almost couldn't recognise them.

Finally he rose, went over to the small pale-wood table, and picked up the seven sheets of rice paper. He crossed the room, passed the half-closed door without turning, and went out.

60.

HERVÉ Joncour in the years that followed chose for himself the serene life of a man with no more needs. He spent his days in the safety of a guarded emotion. In Lavilledieu the people admired him again, because it seemed to them that they saw in him a *precise* way of being in the world. They said that he had been like that even as a young man, before Japan.

With his wife, Hélène, he got into the habit of making, every year, a short journey. They saw Naples, Rome, Madrid, Munich, London. One year they went as far as Prague, where everything seemed: theatre. They travelled without a schedule and without plans. Everything amazed them: secretly, even their happiness. When they felt homesick for silence, they returned to Lavilledieu.

If anyone had asked, Hervé Joncour would have said that they would live like that forever. He had the un-assailable peacefulness of men who feel they are in their place. Every so often, on a windy day, he went through the park to the lake, and stayed there for hours, on the shore, watching the surface of the water ripple, creating unpredictable shapes that sparkled randomly, in all directions. The wind was one alone: but on that mirror of water it seemed thousands, blowing. On every side. A spectacle. Light and inexplicable.

Every so often, on a windy day, Hervé Joncour went to the lake and spent hours watching it, because, drawn on the water, he seemed to see the inexplicable spectacle, light, that had been his life.

61.

ON June 16, 1871, in the back of Verdun's café, before noon, the one-armed player made an irrational four-cushion draw shot. Baldabiou remained leaning over the table, one hand behind his back, the other grasping the cue, incredulous.

'Come on.'

He straightened, put down the cue, and went out without saying anything. Three days later he left. He gave his two silk mills to Hervé Joncour.

'I don't want anything more to do with silk, Baldabiou.'

'Sell them, you fool.'

No one could get out of him where the hell he intended to go. And what he would do there. All he said was something about St Agnes that no one understood very well.

The morning he left, Hervé Joncour, along with Hélène, accompanied him to the train station at

Avignon. He had with him a single suitcase, and this, too, was rather inexplicable. When he saw the train, halted on the track, he put the suitcase down.

'Once I knew someone who had a railroad built all for himself.'

He said.

'And the point of it is that he had it made completely straight, hundreds of miles without a curve. There was also a reason, but I don't remember it. One never remembers the reasons. Anyway: goodbye.'

He wasn't much cut out for serious conversations. And a goodbye is a serious conversation.

They saw him growing distant, him and his suitcase, forever.

Then Hélène did something strange. She separated from Hervé Joncour and ran after him, until she reached him, and hugged him, hard, and as she embraced him she burst into tears.

She never wept, Hélène.

Hervé Joncour sold the two silk mills at a ridiculous price to Michel Lariot, a good fellow who had played dominoes, every Saturday evening, with Baldabiou, always losing, with granite-like consistency. He had three daughters. The first two were called Florence and Sylvie. But the third: Agnès.

62.

THREE years later, in the winter of 1874, Hélène became ill with a brain fever that no doctor could understand, or cure. She died in early March, on a rainy day.

Accompanying her, in silence, on the road to the cemetery, was all Lavilledieu: because she was a happy woman, who had not spread sorrow.

Hervé Joncour had a single word carved on her tombstone:

Hélas.

He thanked everyone, said a thousand times that he needed nothing, and returned to his house. Never had it seemed so large: and never so illogical his fate.

Because despair was an excess that did not belong to him, he submitted to what was left of his life, and began again to look after it, with the unyielding tenacity of a gardener at work the morning after the storm.

63.

Two months and eleven days after Hélène's death, it happened that Hervé Joncour went to the cemetery and found, beside the roses that he laid on his wife's grave every week, a little wreath of tiny blue flowers. He bent down to observe them, and remained in that position for a long time, which from a distance would certainly have appeared, to the eyes of possible witnesses, singular if not ridiculous. Returning home, he didn't go out to work in the park, as he usually did, but stayed in his study, and thought. He did nothing else, for days. Thought.

64.

At 12 Rue Moscat he found a tailor's shop. He was told that Madame Blanche hadn't lived there for years. He managed to find out that she had moved to Paris, where she had become the kept woman of a very important man, perhaps a politician.

Hervé Joncour went to Paris.

It took him six days to find out where she lived. He sent her a note, asking to be received. She answered that she would expect him at four o'clock the next day. Punctually he went up to the second floor of a handsome building on the Boulevard des Capucines. A servant opened the door. She led him to the drawing room and asked him to sit down. Madame Blanche came in wearing a dress that was very stylish and very French. Her hair came down over her shoulders, in the Parisian fashion. She didn't have rings of blue flowers on her fingers. She sat down opposite Hervé Joncour, without a word. And waited.

He looked her in the eyes. But the way a child would have.

'You wrote that letter, right?'

He said.

'Hélène asked you to write it and you did.'

Madame Blanche didn't move; she didn't lower her gaze or betray the least astonishment.

Then what she said was

'It wasn't I who wrote it.'

Silence.

'Hélène wrote that letter.'

Silence.

'She had already written it when she came to me. She asked me to copy it, in Japanese. And I did. That is the truth.'

Hervé Joncour realised at that moment that he would continue to hear those words all his life. He rose, but stood still, as if he had suddenly forgotten where he was going. The voice of Madame Blanche reached him as if from far away.

'She also wanted to read me that letter. She had a beautiful voice. And she read the words with an emotion that I have never been able to forget. It was as if they were, truly, hers.'

Hervé Joncour was crossing the room, with very slow steps.

'You know, *monsieur*, I think that she wished, more than any other thing, *to be that woman*. You can't understand it. But I heard her read that letter. I know that it is so.'

Hervé Joncour had reached the door. He placed his hand on the doorknob. Without turning, he said softly

'Farewell, *madame*.'

They never saw each other again.

65.

HERVÉ Joncour lived for twenty-three more years, most of them in serenity and good health. He never went away from Lavilledieu again, nor did he ever abandon his house. He managed his goods wisely, and that protected him forever from any work that was not the care of his own park. In time he began to yield to a pleasure that in the past he had always denied himself: to those who came to see him, he recounted his travels. Listening to him, the people of Lavilledieu learned about the world, and the children discovered what marvel was. He spoke softly, staring into the air, at things the others couldn't see.

On Sundays he went to town, for High Mass. Once a year he made a tour of the silk mills, to touch the newborn silk. When the solitude wrung his heart, he went to the cemetery, to talk to Hélène. The rest of his time he spent in a liturgy of habits that protected him from unhappiness. Every so often, on a windy day, he went to the lake and spent hours looking at it, because, drawn on the water, he seemed to see the inexplicable spectacle, light, that had been his life.

Ocean Sea

From the author of the international bestseller *Silk*

Alessandro Baricco

CANON‖GATE